DEDICATION

This book is dedicated to my goddaughter Cara Thomas and her wonderful parents, Adam and Emma.

First published in Great Britain in 2024 by Wren & Rook

Text copyright © Dr Alex George 2024
Illustrations copyright © The Boy Fitz Hammond 2024
All rights reserved.

ISBN: 978 1 5263 6667 2

1 3 5 7 9 10 8 6 4 2

Wren & Rook
An imprint of
Hachette Children's Group
Part of Hodder & Stoughton
Carmelite House
50 Victoria Embankment
London EC4Y 0DZ

An Hachette UK Company
www.hachette.co.uk
www.hachettechildrens.co.uk

Printed and bound in Great Britain by Clays Ltd, Elcograf S.p.A.

DR ALEX GEORGE

A Better Day

JOURNAL

Fun and Calming
Activities for
Positive
Mental Health

Illustrated by The Boy Fitz Hammond

CONTENTS

INTRODUCTION

Hi! I'm Dr Alex George, a **medical doctor** and the **Youth Mental Health Ambassador** for the UK government.

When I was growing up, I was a **world-class worrier**. But eventually, I found ways to manage my worries and keep my mind in good shape. I explain how I did this in my first children's book *A Better Day*. But sometimes we also need a place to take a break, build our confidence and write down the things that might be making us feel anxious or sad.

That's where this journal comes in.

This journal is for **YOU!** It's **interactive**, which means you can get your pens and pencils out, scribble all over it, fold the corners – whatever you want to do – while trying out some amazing activities. I want you to make it your own!

It's my hope that this journal will become **like a good friend** who helps you to make each day positive and gives you methods to help look after your mental health with confidence. It is also something you can keep returning to, so you can retrace your steps and go back to the activities in this journal that work for you whenever you need them.

The activities are all based on techniques I've learned from my work as a mental health ambassador, my public mental health master's degree and, probably most important of all, my life! That's not to say that I've got everything sussed – **I'm a work in progress and I'm still learning!** We all are.

You might not get on with all the suggestions, but give them a try, and if you decide something's not working for you, don't fret; skip it and try another one. There are activities to suit everyone – whether you're a wordsmith, an artist or a doodler.

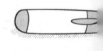

Get CREATive

If you HAVEN'T read A Better Day . . . yet!

OK, I will forgive you this once – but if, after you have completed some of the activities in this book, you want to read more around the **HUGE** topic of mental health and what it all means for you and for everyone you know, I encourage you to get yourself a copy from a local bookshop or library.

If you HAVE read A Better Day . . .

Well, thank you! I hope *A Better Day* has been a game-changer when it comes to understanding your mental health and why being kind to your mind is so important – **not just for you, but for everyone you know and care about.**

We can't control everything that happens around us in our lives. In fact, we can control very little at times! But what we can do is control our actions and reactions to the world around us – both in terms of what's happening in our own heads and also what we do in the 'real' world. Developing and building your mental fitness will help you live a life with confidence, and to go out there and do the things you enjoy while dealing with the obstacles we all inevitably face.

Lastly, before we get started, if you're really struggling, **please ask for help** – there is always support and advice available, and there is always a good reason to hope for **a better day**. I have added some resources to the back of the book on page 142.

Mental health can mean lots of things, and by learning to connect with what's going on inside our minds, we can turn it into a force for good.

PART ONE

MENTAL WELLNESS AND YOU

Let's turn the
page and learn
more about YOU.

All about you

It's time to loosen up by writing down some stuff about you.
See if you can fill in the gaps below. You can doodle all over the
page if you want to – this is your journal and there are no rules!

My name: _____

I look like: (add a photo or draw yourself here!)

My favourite school subject: _____

My least favourite school subject: _____

Things that make my day better: _____

_____

_____

_____

Things I worry about: _____

_____

_____

_____

I am a cat / dog person (delete as appropriate)

My favourite TV show: _____

My favourite music: _____

Are you ready to be kind to your mind?

Then turn the page – it's time for a holiday!

A holiday for your head!

Let's try a visualisation exercise, or, to put it a better way, a holiday for your head! You can **use this exercise whenever things get too much** and you feel like you need to **take a break**. It doesn't involve going somewhere special; you can do it exactly where you are, right now!

Visualisation is all about imagining a scene or an experience in your head. It can be a valuable tool for calming your mind, and scientific studies have shown that it also boosts confidence – even top athletes use this technique to accomplish their goals!

Try to visualise some of these scenes and see if it helps you to feel better. Ready?

Begin by sitting somewhere comfortable and quiet, then close your eyes and imagine you see a beautiful door in front of you. Take a deep breath and then open the door. Your holiday awaits . . .

Imagine seeing your favourite place behind the door. It could be a walk that you like to go on, a park, a beach or even somewhere totally made up – a place where you feel safe, warm, happy and protected, and you have no worries. You can do anything here – you can play, you can rest, you can relax or you can just breathe.

Now you need to use your daydreaming skills to bring your special place to life as much as you can in your mind. To help you build up a picture, on the next page I want you to doodle on the postcard the things that you can see. Then, write down a description, as if you're telling a friend about your holiday on a postcard.

_____

_____

_____

_____

_____

It looks like an incredible place! Now that you have created this holiday in your head, you can come back whenever you feel the need to.

The key to visualisation is to imagine a place where you can feel happy and relaxed. When you change your environment – even if it's just in your head – it can be a powerful way to convince your mind to move beyond your worries and stresses, and to remind yourself that these feelings are only temporary.

A mindful high-five

Everyone is talking about the benefits of mindfulness – you might have learned about it in school. **Mindfulness** is about being in the present moment and feeling connected to the world around us, which can be a big help when we're feeling worried as it calms us down and quietens all those busy thoughts rushing around our minds.

Try this – it's something I first talked about in *A Better Day*. It's an exercise that I like to do when my mind gets too busy.

Ready?

Put any gadgets away, sit comfortably and **press the pause button on your life for the next five minutes**. (Sometimes I even draw a pause button on a sticky note and stick it to my desk. Whenever I feel stressed, I hit the button and take a quick break. Phew!)

Now, simply take notice of the world around you, thinking about your five senses – sight, touch, sound, smell and taste. After five minutes, see if you can fill in the below with what you have noticed!

what are five things you can see?

☆ _____

☆ _____

☆ _____

☆ _____

☆ _____

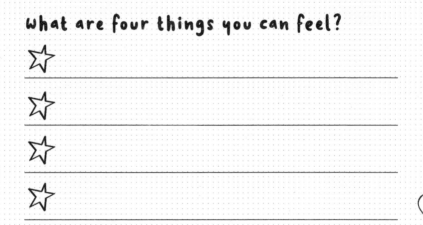

what are four things you can feel?

☆ _____

☆ _____

☆ _____

☆ _____

What are three things you can hear?

☆ _____

☆ _____

☆ _____

What are two things you can smell?

☆ _____

☆ _____

What is one thing you can taste?

☆ _____

Lifeline no. 1:
Make a daily mood journal

How are you feeling today? And how were you feeling yesterday? These are not simple questions when you think about it, are they? We all feel a rainbow of emotions every day, going from happiness, to sadness, to maybe anger or excitement – emotions can be exhausting. It's like the mind is a complex machine with levers and buttons for every emotion, and these levers are always moving in a unique way for all of us.

We are all different – if we weren't, we'd be robots!

Here's a lifeline that will help you to keep track of your mental health, from now until . . . forever!

It's a daily mood journal, and it's so simple. But it could provide vital clues for when you might, say, feel more anxious than normal, or sad or just a bit meh. Writing down what we're thinking and feeling can help us to truly discover what's going on with our mental health – our thoughts have a huge impact on how we feel physically and mentally, and if negative thoughts are taking over, then it's time to do something about it. A mood journal is a handy tool to help you map these emotions over time.

If you are writing something really personal and feel worried about someone finding your innermost thoughts, you don't need to keep these pages. Once you're finished, you're welcome to rip them up, shred them, draw felt-tip pen all over them and destroy them completely! It's up to you.

I sometimes like to write my worries down and then throw them in the bin. **See ya!**

Monday

Today I mostly felt... 😊 ☹️ 😠 😍

Something great that happened: _____

_____

_____

Something not so great that happened: _____

_____

_____

A funny thing that happened: _____

_____

Tuesday

Today I mostly felt... 😊 ☹️ 😠 😍

Something great that happened: _____

_____

_____

Something not so great that happened: _____

_____

_____

A funny thing that happened: _____

_____

Wednesday

Today I mostly felt ... 😊 😞 😠 😍

Something great that happened: _____

_____

_____

Something not so great that happened: _____

_____

_____

A funny thing that happened: _____

_____

Thursday

Today I mostly felt... 🙂 🙁 😠 😍

Something great that happened: _____

_____

_____

Something not so great that happened: _____

_____

_____

A funny thing that happened: _____

_____

Friday

Today I mostly felt... 🙂 🙁 😠 😍

Something great that happened: _____

_____

_____

Something not so great that happened: _____

_____

_____

A funny thing that happened: _____

_____

Saturday

Today I mostly felt... 😊 😟 😠 😍

Something great that happened: _____

_____

_____

Something not so great that happened: _____

_____

_____

A funny thing that happened: _____

_____

Sunday
Today I mostly felt...

Something great that happened: _____

_____

_____

Something not so great that happened: _____

_____

_____

A funny thing that happened: _____

_____

_____

If you run out of
space here, don't worry!
Grab a notebook and keep tracking your
moods, as well as writing down all the great
things that have happened, and all the
not-so-great things.

Let's talk about . . . worry

This is **the big one** for most of us . . . worry. The thing that creeps up on all of us, that stops us in our tracks and can ruin our day.

Worry can affect you mentally and physically in so many ways:

☆ **A feeling of 'butterflies' in your tummy**

☆ **Feeling dizzy and sick**

☆ **Feeling upset and wanting to cry**

☆ **Feeling restless and unable to relax or keep still**

☆ **Feeling sweaty**

☆ **A fast, thumping heartbeat and faster breathing**

☆ **Difficulty sleeping**

☆ **Feeling like you need the toilet more than normal**

It's not a comfortable list, is it? It's likely that you've experienced many of these things at some stage – we all do.

Where does worry strike for you? Imagine this body was your body – can you add in lightning strikes to show where and how worry affects you?

Is it worry or anxiety? What's the difference?

These two words are often used to describe the same thing. All those yucky symptoms listed earlier can occur whether you're experiencing worry or anxiety. So why the two words?

Well, **EVERYONE** experiences low-level worries from time to time; **it's normal and part of being human.**

Anxiety, on the other hand, is a term used to describe **feeling worried for long periods of time**, even when there is no obvious reason to, and it can be very uncomfortable for your mind and your body as you're regularly experiencing adrenaline spikes which make you feel tense, restless and unhappy.

_____

_____

quiet

_____

shaky

The anxiety submarine

Imagine your anxiety as a submarine – a vast vessel bobbing along in the sea. This image shows how our body can display all the obvious signs of anxiety and the not-so-obvious signs beneath the surface.

feeling unhap
in ourselves

**The body of
the submarine**

unhappy in
general

lonely

(the biggest part) represents all the underlying emotions – the things *beneath* the surface.

_____

_____

low self-esteem

_____

_____

34

upset

_____

_____

_____

overthinking   angry

The periscope (the only part of the submarine above the

surface) represents the noticeable signs of anxiety – things like

being quiet or shaky.

Can you think of any other signs? If so, write

them on the blank lines.

_____

worried about
what others think

_____

_____

ot wanting to go
to school

How do we take

control and manage

our anxiety if it's the

size of a submarine?!

We're
going to
need a
lifeline . . .

35

Lifeline no. 2: Open up

It can be difficult to put our thoughts into words and **it takes courage to talk** to someone, especially when we're struggling, so let's break it down into manageable pieces and start with . . .

WHO?

Who do you feel you can speak to? Who do you trust and know will listen without judgement? It could be an older sibling, a trusted adult, like your mum or your teacher, or perhaps a really good friend.

write down three names here:

1. _____

2. _____

3. _____

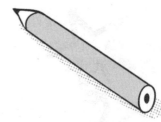

WHERE?

I've found that some of the best conversations I've had have been when I'm sitting in the car and the person I'm talking to is sitting beside me, or when I'm walking with someone, so the pressure is off to look each other in the eye when we might be saying something that's hard to say out loud.

Write your thoughts down here for places and situations that would make you feel most comfortable:

Place 1: _____

Place 2: _____

Place 3: _____

WHEN?

Choosing the right moment is key – pick a time when you're not rushing to get somewhere or finish something.

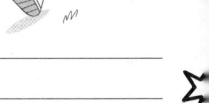

Write your thoughts down here:

_____

_____

HOW?

There are lots of ways to ask for help. Perhaps ask to speak to your chosen trusted person after school or on a quiet Sunday afternoon. If you don't feel confident about saying it, you could send a text or an email, or write a note.

Have a think about your preferred method and write it here:

_____

_____

WHAT?

What do you want to say?

That's a **BIG** question!! And when you're in the moment and your trusted person is ready to listen, it can lead to your mind emptying, like it's suddenly become full of holes!

My advice is to write a few things down beforehand – it could be just a few sentences or keywords that explain how you're feeling. Or even doodles! Whatever works for you.

On the next page have a practise. I've added a few prompts to help, but you don't need to use them.

 I'm struggling with . . .

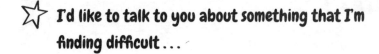 I'd like to talk to you about something that I'm finding difficult . . .

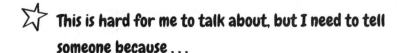 This is hard for me to talk about, but I need to tell someone because . . .

 Do you remember when . . .

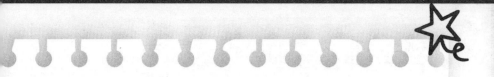

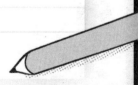

Don't worry if you're not ready to open up just yet – it's not a race.

This is your journey and no one else's.

Also, remember, people who care for us will always want to help.

41

Booster for a better day

Create a chill-out playlist

Well done. You deserve a break as that was hard – or maybe it wasn't – either way, you're **doing great**!

Something I like to do, for a quick five-minute chill, is to listen to a favourite song. I'm quite partial to Taylor Swift, so I'll get my headphones on to block out the day and relax.

Here's a mix tape (what's a mix tape? Ask the nearest oldie!) to fill in with your favourite chill-out tunes.

I'll start and you can fill

in the rest . . .

'Love Story' by Taylor Swift

_____

_____

_____

_____

_____

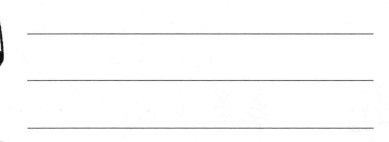

How to turn a negative thought into a positive one

What's the worst that could happen? But what's the best that could happen?

Whenever I did something wrong when I was younger – such as the time I forgot to do my homework – I felt doomed and that the world would hate me forevermore.

But I slowly realised that I could **change my relationship with worry** by turning my negative thoughts into positive ones, and it felt amazing – almost like my very own superpower! Try it yourself. Here's how . . .

Think of something that's been bugging you for ages – perhaps you've got an exam coming up and it's giving you the jitters, or maybe you want to make friends with someone but you're not sure what to say without coming across as a doofus? It could be anything. Got something? Good. There's **ALWAYS** something. Write it below:

My problem: _____

_____

_____

_____

_____

_____

_____

_____

_____

_____

The first thing to ask yourself is:

what is the worst that could happen?

I know, it's not nice to think about, but this is the upside-down of

your problem, the jump-scare of all jump-scares — you can do it!

Write the worst-case scenario here: _____

_____

_____

_____

_____

Then ask yourself:

what's the best that could happen?

Oh, that's a bit nicer, isn't it?

Write your best-case scenario here: _____

_____

_____

_____

_____

And finally, what's most likely to happen?

Write the most-likely scenario here: _____

_____

_____

_____

_____

_____

Well, that's not so bad, is it? If you look back on times when you were brave, the probability of a most-likely or a best-case result was pretty high.

So my advice is to think positive! ♥

Try some positive affirmations

Let's talk a bit more about **thinking positively** and **looking on the bright side**.

Positive affirmations are compliments that you say to yourself, such as **'I am awesome'** and **'I can do this!'**. You might think it's a bit cringe to say these things to yourself, but scientific studies have shown that positive affirmations can help **shift our mindset from a negative to a positive one**.

The trick with affirmations is to use the **present tense** and **refer to yourself in the first person: 'I' or 'my'** – it's a way to awaken your self-belief and give it a shake! Words have power, and kind words can turn a bad day into a great day! Affirmations also have other incredible benefits: they can **boost self-esteem** so you feel ready for something big, like an exam, or they can **soothe away worries** to help you sleep better – incredible!

Here are a few that might work for you – practise saying them in the mirror three times each morning!

I can be anything I want to be.

I am a brilliant friend.

My mind is calm.

I am loved.

Add some of your own positive affirmations to this page with words that have meaning to you.

Make a positive poster!

Think of your favourite affirmation and make a poster on this page – something you can look at and repeat whenever you need to give yourself a lift!

Self-appreciation society!

Sometimes we need to remind ourselves just how brilliant and unique we are.

Because you are **brilliant and unique**!

On the next page, I want you to write down all the things that **make you special** – they could be anything, from being able to make your friends laugh to being brilliant at a specific subject in class.

Come back whenever there is something new to add and **celebrate**.

True or false: Anxiety

It's time to bust some myths about anxiety! See if you can answer these true or false questions correctly. The answers are over the page – no cheating!

	TRUE	FALSE
1. Everyone has anxiety.	☐	☐
2. Anxiety is an illness.	☐	☐
3. There is nothing good about anxiety.	☐	☐
4. Anxiety is just part of life these days.	☐	☐
5. If you have anxiety, you should avoid going to parties.	☐	☐
6. Being anxious is the same as being shy.	☐	☐
7. Everyone can see when you're anxious.	☐	☐

Answers

1: TRUE Everyone has anxiety sometimes – some more than others. It's normal to have some anxiety when faced with a challenging situation.

2: FALSE Anxiety is not an illness – it's a normal part of life. We all have worries. But when worry starts to become unmanageable and takes over your life, it's important to ask for help. (See page 142 for some useful resources.)

3: FALSE Believe it or not, anxiety can be a good thing! It can motivate us to keep going and spur us on, help us stay alert to danger and guide us to solve problems too!

4: FALSE Anxiety goes all the way back to our cave-dwelling ancestors, when there were predators like sabre-toothed tigers who saw us as lunch! It's a natural human stress response that alerts us to potential danger by flooding the body with adrenaline, which sends us into high alert to help us fight or run from predators.

5: FALSE Just because you have anxiety, it doesn't mean you have to miss out on having a good time! Use your lifelines to help you – take a friend who knows you and can support you – and if it gets too much, you don't have to stay.

6: FALSE There is a bit of overlap between shyness and anxiety, but being shy is part of someone's personality, whereas anxiety is something that we all experience.

7: TRUE AND FALSE This is a bit of a trick question. If you go back to page 34 and the anxiety submarine, you'll see there are a lot more symptoms that are under the surface. Everyone experiences anxiety in different ways, and it tends to be our friends and family who can notice when we are feeling anxious, but the average person on the street is unlikely to notice.

Booster for a better day

A moment of calm

Let's relax for a moment.

I have found that one of the simplest things I can do to reach a state of calm when I'm feeling anxious is **breathing**. Yes, you heard it, that thing you do all day, every day! But to make it an effective means to calm yourself, you need to breathe a little differently, by breathing deeply. When you do this, you increase your oxygen levels to the brain, which tells it to chill out – it's so simple and it works!

Try this:

☆ **Relax your shoulders** – give them a little roll if they're stiff.

⭐ **Breathe** in slowly and deeply through your nose to the count of four and feel your lungs fill with air.

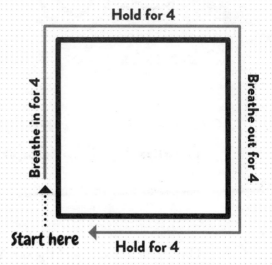

⭐ **Hold** to a count of four.

⭐ **Then purse your lips** and breathe out slowly through your mouth to a count of four.

⭐ **Then hold** for a count of four.

⭐ **Repeat** for a minute or two until you feel calmer.

This is called box breathing, and it's so effective, even the military do it! It helps relieve stress and reduces anxiety when things are particularly difficult, and so the Special Forces have it in their toolbox for when they need to keep calm and think clearly.

Here's another way to calm your breathing – with shapes!

Grab a pen, or just use your finger, to trace the shapes and use

the prompts on each side of the shape.

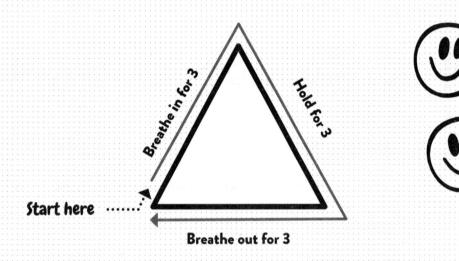

Breathe in for 3

Hold for 3

Start here

Breathe out for 3

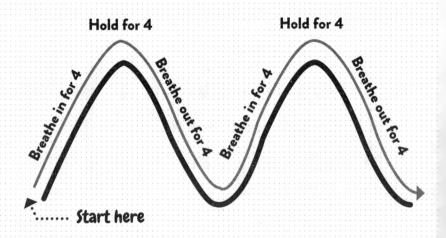

Hold for 4

Hold for 4

Breathe in for 4

Breathe out for 4

Breathe in for 4

Breathe out for 4

Start here

We've reached the end of the first section, where we've talked about **worry** and the tools that you can use to keep it in check, but there is so much more to mental health than dealing with the anxiety submarine.

It's time to look at our minds as a whole and think about how we can maintain and manage our moods and mental fitness in the same way that we exercise our bodies for physical fitness . . .

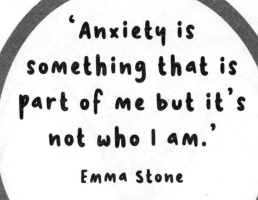

'Anxiety is something that is part of me but it's not who I am.'
Emma Stone

PART TWO

AN INSIDE GUIDE TO YOUR MIND

Let's talk about . . . stress

ARGHHH!!

Stress is a build-up of pressure caused
by the busy lives that we lead – and they are so busy! What's
on your to-do list right now? School? Homework? Calling
your best friend? My to-do list is never-ending! And when it
gets too much, it can leave us feeling tired and
overwhelmed.

Stress is like anxiety in some ways, as it can
also trigger the release of adrenaline, place us
on high alert and make us feel restless. But stress is something
that can also be managed and, believe it or not, it can also be
used in a positive way to get stuff done!

Booster for a better day

Inner smile exercise

This is a really quick exercise that's a great stress reliever and will help to reset your mind, shake off stress and bring a smile to your face.

Smiling on the inside might sound a bit odd, but when we picture in our mind something that makes us smile on the inside – it could be hanging out with a special person, perhaps making some art or having doggy cuddles – we often end up smiling on the outside too!

Close your eyes, imagine something that makes your heart happy and **take three slow, deep breaths**.

Ahh – how did that feel?

Don't get stressed - do something!

Wouldn't it be great if we could pop all our stresses and worries in a box, seal it and post it to outer space? I wish! But here's something you can do to help you to get a grip on them.

What's making you worried and stressed right now? Is it homework, an upcoming test, friendship troubles, annoying siblings, pressure from other people? Have a think and then try the following exercise . . .

One step at a time

When you have a lot of stressful things in your life that demand attention, it can be hard to know where to start. The best thing to do in this case is to break down your to-do list into smaller, more manageable steps.

1. What's my problem? _____

_____

_____

_____

2. What would improve the situation? _____

_____

_____

_____

_____

3. What do I need to do to make this happen?

_____

_____

_____

_____

4. I will solve my problem by: _____

_____

_____

_____

_____

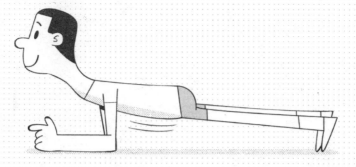

Lifeline no. 3: Get moving!

Whenever I'm stressed, I get active – the gym is my happy place, where I can channel all my frustration into something fun (even if it's a bit sweaty!). Sport and physical activity are essential for our physical and mental wellbeing because:

☆ The endorphins released after exercise feel like a burst of happy energy.

☆ It's a great stress reliever – just try a quick sprint or boxing into the air – it will instantly help you shake off all that tension!

☆ It helps you sleep well – and a good night's sleep plays a vital role in your mental health. Zzzz . . .

☆ Oops, sorry, I drifted off there . . . where was I? Oh yes – exercise also boosts memory function and lengthens attention span.

☆ You will even find it improves your ability to multitask and plan.

☆ It's great for self-confidence and self-esteem.

☆ And most importantly, it keeps you fit and healthy!

There are loads of things you can do – perhaps your school has some sports clubs you could join, or maybe you can arrange to go for a regular run or kickabout in the park with some friends?

READY FOR A CHALLENGE?

I'm going to challenge you to get active for 60 minutes each day. On the next page, think of three activities or sports you can do for a minimum of 20 minutes each day, so you have completed 60 minutes of exercise a day. These can be a mixture of things you do already and other things you'd love to try out. I've filled in the first day for you!

Monday	Tuesday	Wednesday	Thursday	Friday	Saturday	Sunday
Walk to school instead of getting a lift 20 mins						
Do some keepie-uppies and headers in the playground 20 mins						
Dance party! Put on some high-energy songs and dance till you drop! 20 mins						

According to the NHS, children aged five to eighteen should aim for an average of at least 60 minutes of moderate or vigorous intensity physical activity a day across the week. And it's good to mix it up! A variety of sports, with different levels of intensity, helps develop your movement skills, muscles and bones.

Booster for a better day

Go for a stomp!

When I'm feeling a bit off or down in the dumps, one of the most reliable ways to make myself feel better is to pull on my trainers and go outside for a stomp in the fresh air for 20 minutes. Having a furry companion with a waggy tail or a friend to walk with can be great too.

Let's talk about . . . control

Seize the day!

Sometimes it helps to know what we can and can't control, as this enables us to **let go** of the things that we have no power over. It could be things like the weather or something you have heard about on the news, for example. The same applies to other people and their reactions towards us – once we realise these things are out of our hands, it's easier to stop being stressed about them.

Over the page is something called the **circle of influence**.

Everything **inside the circle** is within your control, such as how you act, how you react and the way you treat yourself and others.

Everything **outside the circle** is outside your control, such as how others act, react and behave, the weather, the news and other people's thoughts and feelings.

Thinking about things in this way can be **reassuring and ease your worries**. For example, say you complete a test at school and you try your best – that starts off inside the circle because how you perform in your test is within your control.

Once you have done your test and it's gone to the teacher to be marked, it's outside of your circle of influence and no longer in your control. Once you realise that the thing that you are worried about is something outside of your circle of influence, you can learn not to worry about it.

Things I can't control

politics

bad things in the news

what other people
think of me

the future

weather

other people's
feelings

self-care

how I behave

my values

how I treat others

my boundaries

Things I can control

See if you can add any more examples to the diagram.

Booster for a better day

Watch a film!

It's so important to be kind to your mind and give yourself a break, especially when you're stressed. One thing that always gives me a mood lift and helps me to relax is watching a film.

Write down some of your favourites here:

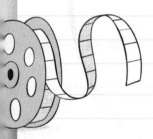

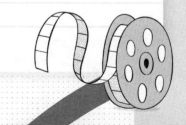

Reboot and get creative

Sometimes we can feel low. It could be that we've had a setback or disappointment, or we're stressed or tired, or for no reason at all. It sucks! But one thing you can do to give your mind a reboot is to get creative.

Here's my challenge to you . . .

Have you heard of **Hirameki**? It's the Japanese art of doodling, and the word means 'flash of inspiration'. It's designed to get your creativity fired up! Hirameki works by giving you random blobs and shapes as prompts and invites you to imagine these blobs into familiar shapes by doodling on them – it's kind of like cloud-watching with a pen.

Here are some blobs I prepared earlier! I want you to draw them into dogs of every shape, breed and size that you can imagine – invent new ones if you want to – the only limit is your imagination. If you're more of a cat person, turn to the following page!

OK, cat lovers, it's your turn!

I hope that's given you a mood-lift!

If you're lucky enough to have a furry and four-pawed member of your family, pets can be another great lifeline when you need comfort, or to simply get you up and out of the house for walkies. My dog, Rolo Polo (named after my favourite sweet and a bit of rhyming made up by my mum!) has changed my life. My morning walks with Rolo help me to connect with nature, get my heart beating and clear my mind. They set me up for the day.

Don't have a dog? Don't worry. Why not ask your grown-ups if you can start going on a short walk each day – it could be to the local park or just round the block for some fresh air.

Booster for a better day

Try something new!

Low mood can make us feel stuck and empty and wrong, like the spinning wheel of doom on a computer screen, but it's whirring inside our brain instead – eugh!

When you find yourself feeling like this, my advice is to try something new! It could be anything – making a friendship bracelet, learning a new skill, joining a club or trying a new sport – because whatever you do, it will activate the happy hormone, dopamine, and you will feel instantly better.

What new things could you try? Why not give yourself the challenge of doing something new every day for a week? Write down the 'something new' in the diary on the next page when you have done it and draw an emoji underneath that best describes your mood afterwards. Good luck!

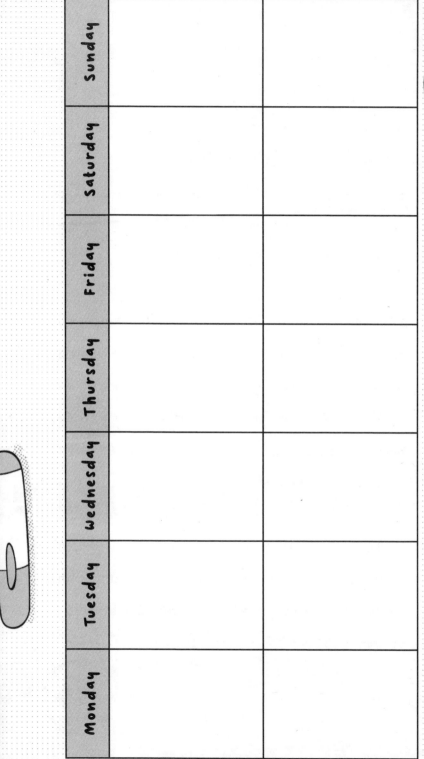

Monday	Tuesday	Wednesday	Thursday	Friday	Saturday	Sunday

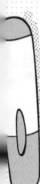

Lifeline no. 4: Keep a daily gratitude journal

What do we mean by gratitude? It sounds like a fuddy duddy word that oldies use, doesn't it? But it's **hot news** as it's a great thing to do for your **mental wellness**.

So what is all the fuss about and what is it? **Gratitude journaling is simply the habit of recording the things that you are grateful for.** How is that different to journaling, you might ask? Well, it gives you the opportunity to **reflect on your day and your life and where you are right now** by writing down the things that make you smile and feel good. It's often three things. Some examples could be:

1. I'm grateful for my doggy cuddles in the morning.
2. I'm thankful the sun was shining and I got to play in the park with my friends.
3. I'm grateful for the people that love and support me.

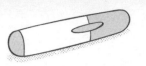

The habit of writing down three good things every day and pausing to reflect on these things has been proven to boost positive mental wellbeing. What's more, psychological research into gratitude journaling has found that it can **rewire your brain!** Woah!

That's because thinking about and appreciating all the positive things in our lives boosts the production of serotonin – which is our stress-reliever chemical – and dopamine – our happy chemical – so that means . . .

Thinking happy thoughts makes you happier and healthier!

Here are some pages of a gratitude journal to get you started. Once you've made it into a habit, get yourself a special notebook and keep going!

It's up to you when you fill in the journal – it could be at the start of the day, or it could be part of your bedtime routine.

Gratitude Journal

Date: _____

Three things that made today great:

1. _____
   _____

2. _____
   _____

3. _____
   _____

Affirmation of the day: _____
_____

Today I am grateful for:
_____
_____
_____

Tomorrow I am looking forward to:
_____
_____
_____

Gratitude Journal

Date:_____

Three things that made today great:

1._____

_____

2._____

_____

3._____

_____

Affirmation of the day: _____

_____

Today I am grateful for:

_____

_____

_____

Tomorrow I am looking forward to:

_____

_____

_____

Gratitude Journal

Date: _____

Three things that made today great:

1. _____
_____

2. _____
_____

3. _____
_____

Affirmation of the day: _____
_____

Today I am grateful for:

_____
_____
_____

Tomorrow I am looking forward to:

_____
_____
_____

Let's talk about . . . resilience

What do you think resilience means?

Resilience, in a nutshell, is when you show grit and determination when life gets difficult. It's also having the self-belief to bounce back from disappointments or bumps in the road.

Everyone has been through disappointments, even (and especially!) hugely successful stars, like one of my personal favourites, Sir Lewis Hamilton. He went through countless setbacks and crashes (literal ones!) before becoming a Formula 1 World Champion.

Sometimes it helps to talk to an older person – it could be an older sibling, a teacher or one of the oldies in your family – and ask them about a difficult time in their life and how they got through it. I have a tattoo that says **'What if I fall? Oh, but my darling, what if you fly?'** It reminds me to always believe in myself and to keep trying, even when times are tough.

It's time for **Dr Alex Investigates** . . .

Grab the mic (OK, a hairbrush will do!),

ask your chosen older person the following

questions and write down their answers . . .

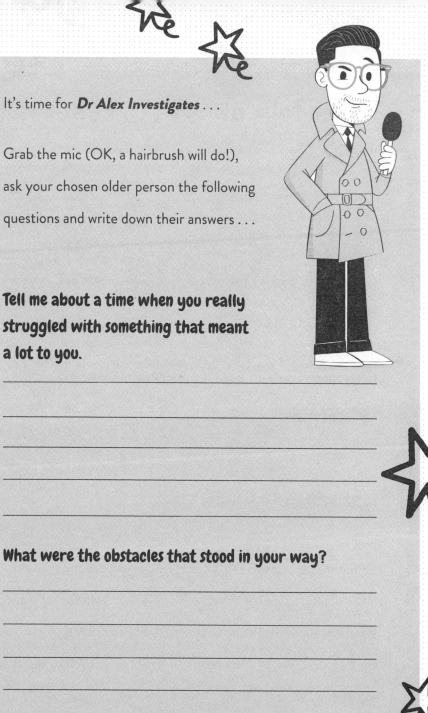

**Tell me about a time when you really
struggled with something that meant
a lot to you.**

_____

_____

_____

_____

_____

What were the obstacles that stood in your way?

_____

_____

_____

_____

_____

Were you frightened of failing?

_____

_____

_____

_____

How did you cope with the setbacks?

_____

_____

_____

_____

_____

What motivated you to try again?

_____

_____

_____

_____

_____

_____

What three qualities do you think will help me when I face a challenging situation?

1. _____

2. _____

3. _____

That was fun! Hopefully you have some great tips from your chosen interviewee.

Remember: when you're faced with a challenging situation, you don't have to deal with it alone. There's a saying that goes **'a problem shared is a problem halved'** and it's true – sharing a problem can help you to come up with solutions together, and you're guaranteed to feel so much better knowing that someone else is on your side.

Sometimes picking yourself up again after a disappointment can be really hard, and you might just want to roll into a duvet burrito for a while and hide, and that's OK. When you're ready to deal with the problem, remember to use your lifelines!

Booster for a better day

Breathing exercise: Dessert time!

I want you to draw the most delicious **hot** dessert below.

Mine would be apple crumble with custard – yum!

Once you've drawn it, you need to take a deep breath in through your nose – imagine you're smelling that sweet dessert! – and then blow out through your mouth as if blowing on the dessert to cool it down. Do this five times, and then drop your shoulders and relax.

Learning from mistakes

Allow me to let you into a little secret: when you become an adult, you make just as many mistakes as when you were a kid. There, I've said it! And, what's more, it's no big deal. Why? Because it gets easier the more mistakes you make, and **the key to overcoming them is to learn from them**. This type of learning is described as having a '**growth mindset**'.

Making mistakes can feel hard and uncomfortable sometimes, but it's how everyone learns – just think, we were all babies once, and we couldn't feed ourselves or walk or wash ourselves, and look at us now! All the things we have learned, we have done through trial and error, and plenty of slip-ups, scuffed knees and cringe moments!

On the next page, see if you can circle the true statements about growth mindset.

True or false: Growth mindset

I won't get better at this.

I will get better at this.

This is too hard.

I can give it a try.

I'm stuck.

I'm doomed!

I'll keep practising and I will improve.

I give up.

Maybe I can try a different way.

There's no other way.

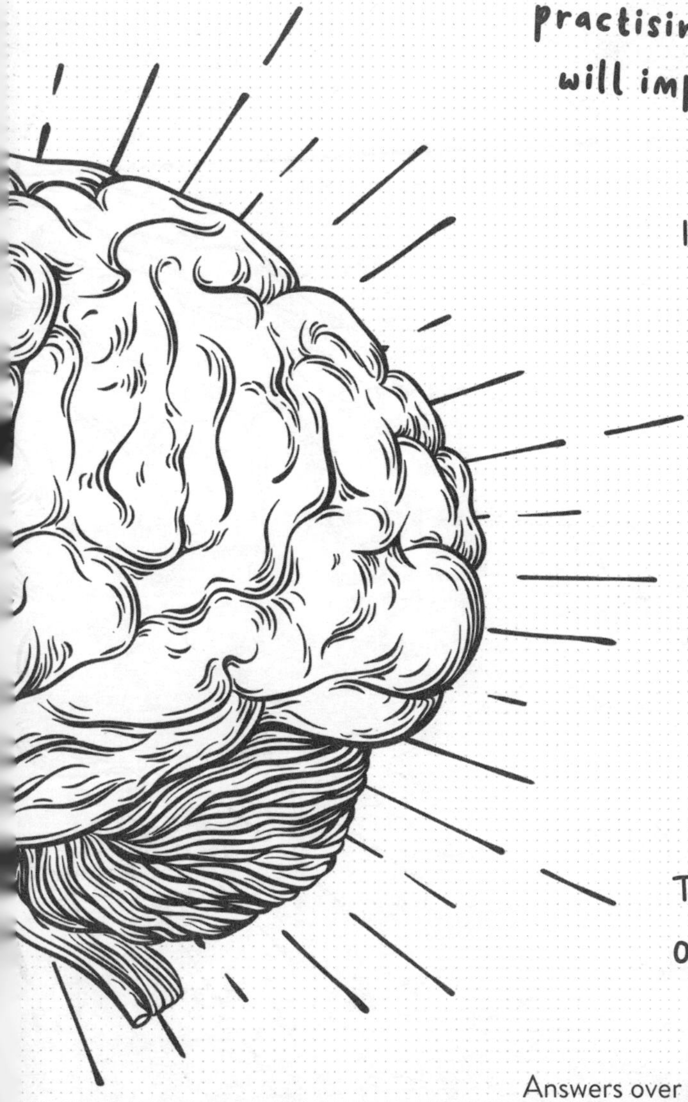

Answers over the page!

Answers:

True growth mindset statements

☆ *I will get better at this.*

☆ *I can give it a try.*

☆ *I'll keep practising and I will improve.*

☆ *Maybe I can try a different way.*

The rest were what we call fixed mindset statements. And don't worry – we all have moments when we want to give up.

When I didn't do as well as I expected in my medical exams, I felt rubbish, and I could have just stopped right there and given up, but, instead, I used one of my lifelines: I spoke to my family, and they encouraged me to try again.

The truth is, I couldn't have done it on my own, and I'm so glad to have been given that extra push to achieve my dreams!

Keep going! You're doing great! ♥

Be kind to your mind

It's time for some 'me time'. Nope, I haven't just made a grammatical error. 'Me time' is time just for me, or **YOU** in this case. It's so important to allow yourself time to relax and do something you enjoy to keep your mind healthy and happy.

Here's my list of things I like to do during 'me time':

☆ Put my gadgets away

☆ Listen to some songs

☆ Cuddle my dogs

☆ Chat to my best friend

☆ Practise my favourite hobbies

Write your list here: _____

_____

_____

_____

_____

_____

Be the reason someone smiles today

It's lovely having people say nice things to us and do lovely things for us, but scientific evidence has shown that there are some big mental health benefits in doing things for others too!

When we're kind to others, it has a **positive effect on their mental health** and in turn has a **positive effect on our mental health too**, so it's a win-win!

You could be an important lifeline to someone else someday.

Name some people in your life who have been kind to you:

1. _____

2. _____

3. _____

What kind of things could you do for them?

Remember: an important part of being kind is considering that person's feelings, so it's important that your act of kindness is something that the other person will find helpful.

Here are some ideas for kind things that you could do:

☆ Check in with a friend and ask them how they're doing

☆ Share your skills and talents with others

☆ Get in touch with a friend or relative that you haven't spoken to for a while

☆ Tell someone just how much you appreciate them

☆ Offer to help with chores

☆ Offer encouragement when someone really needs it

And if you're online, make sure you're kind there too! If you're going to say something, always question whether you would like that to be said about you or whether you would say it to that person's face. If you wouldn't, don't post it.

For this person: _____

I can: _____

_____

_____

_____

_____

Being kind to others is being kind to yourself.

For this person: _____

I can: _____

_____

_____

For this person: _____

I can: _____

_____

_____

For this person: _____

I can: _____

_____

_____

For this person: _____

I can: _____

_____

_____

'Life is so much easier when you're nice.'

Dwayne 'The Rock' Johnson

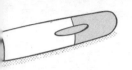

LIFELINES

Lifeline no. 5: Get creative!

I've shared a few ideas for **unleashing your creativity** in this book, but let's look at why it's a lifeline. Before we start, it's important to know that you don't have to be a genius at art or music, or whatever, to enjoy the benefits of being creative. Phew, that's a relief!

When we get absorbed into a creative pursuit, whether it's colouring-in, doodling dogs, painting or baking a cake, for example, we experience **a state of flow**. Flow is what happens when you're focusing on the task to such an extent that the outside world appears to melt away and your worries along with it. It also improves brain function by activating different areas of your mind – wow!

So how do we find our flow? Over the next few pages, there are some creative activities to get you in the flow – enjoy!

A drawing a day

I want you to imagine a world without smartphones and gadgets for a moment. Let's assume that if you wanted to record an image, you would have to draw it. So for every day this month (yes, month!) I want you to draw something that you want to remember – a memory that you would like to record forever, like a different screensaver image for each day.

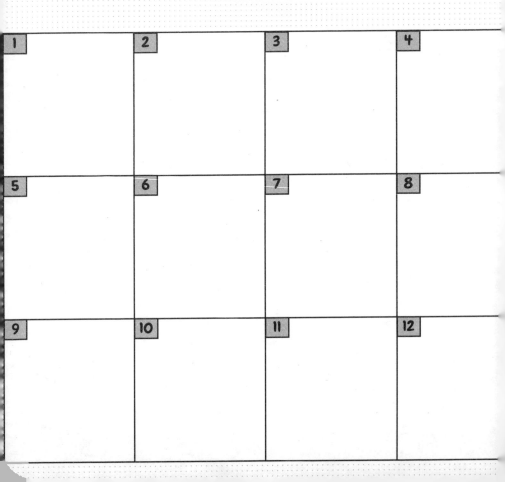

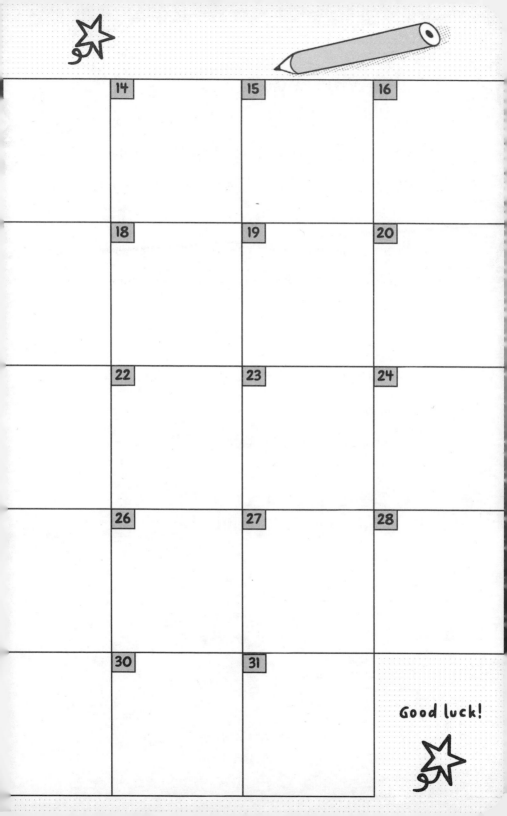

	14	15	16
	18	19	20
	22	23	24
	26	27	28
	30	31	Good luck!

Flow-doodler

This is a fun activity, and it's a bit silly too – but trust me, it's worth it! Get into the flow with some of your favourite music – it could be a bit of Flo Rida (see what I did there?!) or anything that you love to listen to that makes you want to move.

Now grab a pencil and hit **PLAY!**

Place your pencil on the dot on the opposite page and move it around the page as you listen to the music. You can do this with your eyes closed if you want.

It's not a competition; it's just for fun!

104

We've reached the end of part two, where we've talked about **growth mindset, being creative, trying something new, being kind**, learning to be **resilient and lots more!** Let's move on and look at what we can do to feel positive and happier every day.

PART THREE

A BETTER DAY

Let's talk about . . . being happy

See what you think of these statements about happiness – which of them are true?

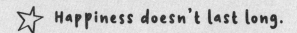 Happiness is something you are born with.

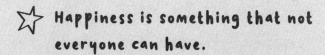 Happiness doesn't last long.

 Happiness is never feeling sad or lonely.

Happiness is something that not everyone can have.

OK, I've tricked you a little here, because all those statements are false! Happiness is something that everyone can have, but you must work at it! The Boosters for a better day and other activities in this chapter will give you the tools to **grow** your happiness.

In fact, grow is a good word for happiness – imagine your happiness is a plant. What does a plant need to thrive and grow?

> 'Don't try so hard to fit in, and certainly don't try so hard to be different . . . just try hard to be you.'
>
> Zendaya

Draw a plant in the pot and add the following tags: fresh air, daylight, water, nutrients. Can you think of any more?

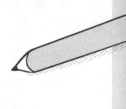

What extras did you think of? Any of these: space, support and love? Do you see the connection between what you need to thrive and to be happy and what a plant needs?

All the things I love about me

It's time to flex – **what are the things that you love most about yourself**? It's not showing off, because this list is for **you**. It's your gallery of achievements so that when something happens to trip you up, you can come back to this page and remind yourself just what a talented, unique and brilliant person you are!

I have these unique talents:

1. _____

2. _____

3. _____

4. _____

5. _____

6. _____

7. _____

8. _____

My proudest achievements at school this year are:

1. _____

2. _____

3. _____

4. _____

5. _____

6. _____

I'm the only person I know that can:

_____

_____

_____

_____

_____

It's important to give yourself a little pat on the back every so often, just to remind yourself that you're doing great!

Compliments

A compliment is a kind thing you can say to someone that can make their day, week or even year! If someone says you're a good friend, for example, that's huge!

It can feel a bit embarrassing when the spotlight is on you, can't it? But the happy hormones released can leave you buzzing – and it's great. How do we capture that buzz? Well, here's your chance. The next time someone pays you a compliment, write it down inside one of the bees on these pages. Yep, this is your gallery of compliments so you can re-read them to feel that happy buzz again!

Be sure to give compliments too; they will mean the world to the people you say them to.

Be inspired by others

Here are some great quotes from big thinkers that I like to have in my back pocket whenever I'm having a bad day and I need a mental boost. Which words chime with you? Perhaps you have heard something and it made you stop and think? If so, write it down.

'This too shall pass.'
Marcus Aurelius

'If your dreams don't scare you, they are too small.'
Richard Branson

_____
_____
_____
_____
_____

'Don't let anyone tell you what you can or cannot do, or cannot achieve. Do not allow it.'
Emma Watson

'If you hear a voice within you say "you cannot paint," then by all means paint and that voice will be silenced.'
Vincent Van Gogh

'You can achieve anything in life, so long as you put your mind to it.'
My mum

Find a mentor

A mentor is someone you look up to: a person who you aspire to be like and makes you strive to be the best version of yourself. It could be someone who you know personally – a parent or grandparent, for example – or perhaps it's someone who has achieved great success in their chosen profession, like a footballer or a singer.

Pick someone who has had a positive impact on you:

Draw them here –
make it flattering!

Now I want you to do some research on this person. What were they like and what were they doing when they were your age? This is much easier when it's someone you know and can ask. But if you don't know them, there's lots of information online and in books, so with the help of your adult, you can search and find out.

It can really help to see where someone has started and the journey they made to get where they wanted to be, because the likelihood is that they had to work really hard. **Write down your findings here:** _____

_____

_____

_____

_____

_____

_____

_____

Next, I want you to find out their educational path, and then the stepping stones they have taken to be successful.

_____

_____

_____

_____

Finally, I want you to imagine what you'd like to say to that person. Or, if it's someone you don't know, imagine what you would say to them if you had the chance. Write them a letter and remember to tell them why they are such an inspiration.

_____

_____

_____

_____

_____

_____

_____

_____

_____

_____

_____

_____

_____

_____

_____

_____

_____

_____

_____

_____

_____

_____

_____

_____

If you're feeling brave, I want you to give them the letter, or post it to them and see what happens!

Lifeline no. 6: Enjoy nature

We are all part of nature, and it can often be easy to forget this when we're hunched over our devices or schoolbooks. There's a whole world out there waiting to be explored, right on your doorstep! The best part is that nature is free to enjoy and has loads of benefits for your mental and physical wellbeing.

Here are just a few of nature's benefits.

It has a calming effect, helping to lower blood pressure and stress.

It's a mood-booster be out in the fresh air

It can inspire creativity with its beauty.

Sunshine gives you vital vitamin D!

It helps you to be more present and feel less anxious.

Go outside, take a deep
breath and draw the animals
and plants you can see.

Lifeline no. 7: Friends

The great thing about friendships is that you can choose them, and not only are good friends great fun to hang out with, but a healthy friendship is also one where there is **respect, trust and kindness.**

GOOD

NOT SO GOOD

Friends don't grow on trees and you must nurture your friendships; being a good friend is an important life skill. So what do you think makes a good friend, and which qualities are not so good in a friend? **Draw a line from each of the below traits to the category you think it belongs in.**

☆ Disagrees with me
☆ Puts themselves first
☆ Is kind
☆ Doesn't like the same team
☆ Listens to me when I have a problem
☆ Makes me happy
☆ Makes me sad
☆ Is fun to spend time with
☆ Criticises how I look
☆ Remembers things I've said
☆ Gossips about me to others
☆ Is always competing with me
☆ Doesn't listen
☆ Wants me to dress like them
☆ Calls me all the time

How did you get on? There were a couple of trick ones in there, but I hope it was obvious which were the negative traits – the ones that would make you feel criticised or unhappy, which could take a toll on your self-esteem. If you feel like a friend is not being a good friend and it's affecting you, open up to one of your trusted lifelines.

The most important message of all is to make friends with people that like you for you.

It's OK to see things differently – maybe you're a cat person and your friend is a dog lover, and that's OK! As long as you have a healthy respect for your differences.

And hey, don't beat yourself up if you recognise a negative trait in yourself. Remember: **you have a growth mindset, and you can learn and grow to become better!**

Look for LOLs

Sometimes, to have a better day, we just need to have a **good laugh**. Laughter makes us feel good – it boosts oxygen in our blood, increases blood circulation and untenses our muscles so that we feel relaxed. A big belly laugh – you know the sort, where you're clutching your stomach as if it might burst – even serves as a workout for your stomach muscles! **Laughter is the opposite of feeling stressed**, as it activates the part of our nervous system that encourages rest and relaxation. And it's a great way to connect with others by sharing or experiencing something that makes us laugh together.

Can you make a list of times when you've rolled around on the floor with laughter? Here are some of mine:

Being silly and childish with my best friend. Adam.

Watching Shrek 2.

Scaring my assistant. Abby.

When I did a pram race on a popular TV show and tripped and fell (dolls in prams obvs).

Write yours here:

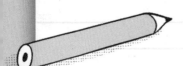

Remembering these funny memories could lead to even more LOLs.

Laughter therapy

One of the best times you can have with your friends is when you have a good giggle. Try this laughter therapy practice together and see who cracks up first!

Stand in a circle if there are a few of you, or opposite each other if it's you and one other.

Take some deep breaths in and out – in through your nose and out through your mouth.

Loosen up with a few stretches – you need to get limber because you're about to get a laughter workout!

HA!

HA!
HA!

Start chuckling quietly – see if you can mimic one another. You could even try different laughter styles in your group – there's always someone with an outrageous laugh that sounds like a sea lion!

Chuckle more loudly with your mouth wide and smiling.

Now let go, laugh as hard as you can and feel your belly tense and release!

Need a quick booster but not with a group of friends? The act of smiling can actually trick your brain into thinking you're relaxed and happy, and lift your mood. So even if you don't feel like it, pull a really big grin and see how it feels!

Lifeline no. 8: Sleep

It's time for a nap after all that exertion. Zzz ... Sleep plays a vital role in maintaining our mental and physical wellbeing. It is crucial to allow your body and mind to rest, restore and grow, so that when you wake up in the morning, you feel ready to take on the challenges of a new day.

Here are my tips for a good night's sleep:

Get the hours in: According to sleep experts,* when you're going to school and are under thirteen years old, you need between nine and twelve hours' sleep every night. If you're over thirteen, you need between eight and ten hours' sleep each night. That's a lot of sleep!

Build a sleep routine: Aim to do something relaxing and nothing too taxing before you go to bed. Perhaps read a few pages of a book, write in your gratitude journal (see page 80) or have a warm bath – or all three! Whatever it takes to get your mind to unwind.

*thesleepcharity.org.uk

Write down your worries: If you have any lingering worries it can help to write them down so they're out of your head. I like keeping a little notepad by the side of my bed.

Be prepared: It can also help to prepare anything for the next day, such as making sure your homework is in your bag, finished, and your clothes aren't all scrunched up on the floor – yes, you know who you are!

Put away phones and tech: If you have a phone, make sure it's out of the room. If you need an alarm, either get your grown-ups to give you a wake-up call or ask for an old-fashioned alarm clock.

Stick to a routine: Our bodies and minds thrive on routine and if you get in the habit of going to bed and getting up at the same time every day, you will feel tired when it's time for bed and recharged and ready to go when it's getting-up time.

Write down your new sleep routine here and see if you can stick to it: _____

_____

_____

_____

_____

_____

_____

_____

_____

_____

_____

_____

_____

_____

_____

ZZZZ

Sleep tracker

Here's a tracker to record your hours of sleep, your morning energy levels, your morning mood and your bedtime routine. It can help you to check in on the times when you don't sleep so well. If you are having difficulty sleeping, don't forget to use a lifeline. Shade the shapes in to show how much you slept and how much energy you had.

Hours Slept

MONDAY	TUESDAY	WEDNESDAY	THURSDAY	FRIDAY	SATURDAY	SUNDAY
12 10 8 6 4 2	12 10 8 6 4 2	12 10 8 6 4 2	12 10 8 6 4 2	12 10 8 6 4 2	12 10 8 6 4 2	12 10 8 6 4 2

Energy

Mood

	MONDAY	TUESDAY	WEDNESDAY	THURSDAY	FRIDAY	SATURDAY	SUNDAY
🙂	☐	☐	☐	☐	☐	☐	☐
☹️	☐	☐	☐	☐	☐	☐	☐
😠	☐	☐	☐	☐	☐	☐	☐
😍	☐	☐	☐	☐	☐	☐	☐

Before Bed

	MONDAY	TUESDAY	WEDNESDAY	THURSDAY	FRIDAY	SATURDAY	SUNDAY
📱	☐	☐	☐	☐	☐	☐	☐
🎧	☐	☐	☐	☐	☐	☐	☐
🍶	☐	☐	☐	☐	☐	☐	☐
📖	☐	☐	☐	☐	☐	☐	☐

A Better Day first-aid kit

Hopefully you will now have a good idea of the things that you need to have a better day – so why not make your own *A Better Day* first-aid kit? A box full of positive things that you can grab in times of need.

Here are some questions to consider when deciding what to place in your *A Better Day* first aid kit:

☆ **What makes you feel happy?**

☆ **What things do you like to see, hear, smell, taste and touch that make you feel happy?**

☆ **What object brings you comfort and make you feel happy?**

Put your answers into your own *A Better Day* first-aid kit on page 136.

The things I would have in my kit might sound a bit strange to you, but these always make me feel calm:

Freshly cut grass – the smell takes me back to childhood in Wales, surrounded by fields and countryside. Every summer the grass would be cut and harvested. Whenever I smell it, I think of those amazing memories with family.

I'd also have a photo of Rolo, some Hobnob biscuits as a treat and my favourite big cosy hoodie.

I find white noise calming too – such as the sound of a hairdryer! So I'd have one of those in my kit as well.

Once you've decided what is going in your first-aid kit, why not make one for real! You could decorate an old shoebox and keep it beneath your bed until you need a boost.

A better day for everyone!

We've reached the end of your journal! Well, almost. Before I go, I want to talk about ways you can help others to feel more positive every day.

In the final section of *A Better Day*, I talked about my idea for a Wellness Sports Day, to help everyone live their best lives. I want mental health support to be available for everyone, and you, yes, **YOU** can help spread the word!

Take a look at these ideas – I want you to see how many you can do in a school term and tick off each challenge as and when you have achieved it.

Good luck!

Get talking about the benefits of mental wellness:

1. Talk to a teacher about the importance of mental health support. ☐
2. Suggest some activities from this book to do as a class. ☐
3. Chat with your friends about wellness and what it means. ☐
4. Do a show-and-tell for your class on one of the topics covered in this book. ☐

Try out some Booster activities from this book with your class:

1. Give Hirameki a go. ☐
2. Do a mindful high-five. ☐
3. Go for a stomp. ☐
4. Create your *A Better Day* first-aid kit. ☐

Plan a Wellness Sports Day:

1. Work with your teacher to curate a plan. ☐

2. Try a post-lunch mindful mediation. ☐

3. Challenge everyone to the anxiety quiz. ☐

4. Create 'holiday for your head' postcards and pin them up on the wall. ☐

5. Interview your teacher about growth mindset! ☐

Invent your own wellness events!

See if you can come up with your own exercises.

Write them below:

_____

_____

_____

_____

_____

_____

Draw and make rosettes and badges with positive affirmations to share and wear during your Wellness Sports Day!

I am worthy.
I am loved.
I love me

Goodbye, for now!

Looking after your mental health is a lifelong commitment, and it's my hope that the tools you've learned about in this book will last you a lifetime – as well as being fun. You don't need to wait for a down day to enjoy these activities!

Just remember to **make looking after your mind as important as looking after your body** by checking in with your feelings, using your lifelines when you need them and setting time aside each day for a Booster activity, such as going for a stomp, mood and gratitude journaling and finding calm through creativity. With these simple steps, we can always enjoy a better day.

Life throws us into the deep end at times, however, with the help of family and friends, we can overcome even the most seemingly insurmountable challenges.

Lifeline no. 9: Help and resources

UK

CALM thecalmzone.net
Runs campaigns to raise awareness and challenge the stigma that stops people talking about suicide and asking for help.

Childline childline.org.uk
Offers a free, confidential service for young people to talk to counsellors via phone, online chat or email.

Heads Together headstogether.org.uk
Works to challenge the stigma around mental health and to help people open up and ask for help.

Hub of Hope hubofhope.co.uk
A database of local and national mental health support and services.

Mental Health Mates mentalhealthmates.co.uk
A network of peer support groups run by people who are experiencing their own mental health issues. They meet regularly to walk, talk and share their experiences without judgement.

Mind mind.org.uk
Provides mental health advice and support, and campaigns to raise awareness and improve services.

Samaritans samaritans.org
Offers listening and support services over the phone or on email.

Switchboard switchboard.lgbt
Provides support and information via an LGBTQ+ helpline, including phone, email and online chat services.

The Proud Trust theproudtrust.org/young-people
Provides help and resources for LGBTQ+ young people.

Australia

Kids Helpline kidshelpline.com.au
A free, confidential 24/7 online and phone counselling service for young people aged five to twenty-five in Australia.

New Zealand

Youthline youthline.co.nz
Provides support to young people aged twelve to twenty-four in New Zealand, including a 24/7 helpline (via phone, email, text and webchat).

India

The MINDS Foundation mindsfoundation.org
An organisation based in India which works to remove the stigma around mental health illnesses and improve access to care.

South Africa

LifeLine lifelinesa.co.za
Offers a 24/7 phone counselling service to anyone in South Africa who is struggling, and aims to improve emotional wellness.

QUOTE SOURCES

Emma Stone in 'Emma Stone discusses her struggled with anxiety . . .' YouTube. 25 March 2022. https://www.youtube.com/watch?v=ixZSYCECsww, accessed 15 August 2023. **Dwayne Johnson.** 'How Dwayne Johnson Became the World's Biggest Star.' 13 July 2018. https://www.forbes.com/sites/forbesdigitalcovers/2018/07/12/why-the-rocks-social-media-muscle-made-him-hollywoods-highest-paid-actor/, accessed 15 August 2023. **Zendaya.** X. 27 January 2015. https://twitter.com/Zendaya/status/560192945429557249?lang=en-GB, accessed 15 August 2023. **Richard Branson.** Facebook. 19 July 2017. https://www.facebook.com/RichardBranson/posts/dream-big-if-your-dreams-dont-scare-you-they-are-too-small-httpsvirgin4kz-future/10154829636965872/, accessed 15 August 2023.**Marcus Aurelius.** *Meditations.* Penguin Classics, 2006. **Emma Watson** in a live Facebook web chat. March 2015. https://www.harpersbazaar.com/uk/people-parties/people-and-parties/news/a36308/emma-watsons-10-most-empowering-quotes/, accessed 15 August 2023. **Vincent van Gogh** quoted on VincentvanGogh.org.

Also Available:

Practical and friendly advice from...
DR ALEX GEORGE

A Better Day

Your Positive Mental Health Handbook

illustrated by
The Boy Fitz Hammond